the Legend of

KEVIN

BY THE REMARKABLE DOUBLE ACT THAT IS

PHILIP REEVE
AND
SARAH McINTYRE

OXFORD
UNIVERSITY PRESS

This is Kevin.

Kevin is a flying pony. (You may have noticed that already, in which case you are Very Observant. Well done! Award yourself 1 gold star.)

Some people think Kevin is a slightly odd shape for a flying pony. They say that his wings are a bit too small. They also say his tummy is a bit too big.

Kevin disagrees
—he thinks he is Just Right.

Kevin lives in the wild, wet hills of the Outermost West, where he has built a large, untidy nest for himself in the branches of an oak tree. His favourite things to eat are:

1. Grass

2. Apples

3. Biscuits

. . . only not in that order.

Grass is quite easy to come by, because it grows all over the wild, wet hills of the Outermost West. Apples grow on the trees in the orchards, and Kevin often flies down to eat them. (You can imagine how delighted the farmers are when they see him coming.) Biscuits are a bit harder to get hold of, but sometimes Kevin makes friends with a hiker, and if he's lucky they share their biscuits with him. So if ever you visit the wild, wet hills of the Outermost West, be sure to take plenty of biscuits. Kevin's favourites are:

1. Pink wafers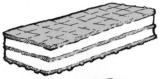

2. Bourbons

3. Custard creams

. . . only not in that order.

ONE

KEVIN BLOWS AWAY

One night there was a terrible storm. It blew across the Outermost Sea, where the mermaids lived. It drove huge white waves against the black rocks where gangs of cheeky Sea Monkeys made their homes. It howled over the wild, wet hills. Kevin huddled down in his treetop nest and squeezed his eyes tight shut against the rain. The wind blew harder and harder. It lashed Kevin's oak tree to and fro until the nest fell out of its branches and Kevin fell out of the nest.

Kevin flapped his small wings as fast as they would flap, but the wind was too strong for him. It carried him high into the sky. It blew him far across the wild, wet hills. It blew him over roads and rivers, all the way to the places where ordinary people lived—people who didn't believe in flying ponies.

He blew past
electricity pylons and
mobile phone masts
and forests of chimneys,
until at last, with a loud
DOOF, he bumped into the
side of a tall building.
'Bother!' said Kevin.

Inside the tall building there lived a short boy. The boy's name was Max, and he looked like this:

Max lived in the flat on the top floor of the tall building, with his mum and dad and sister.

Max's dad was a builder. He was very good at it. Wherever Max went in the little town of Bumbleford there were roofs that his dad had fixed, or porches that he had put up, and even whole houses he had built. Max was proud of that.

Max's mum was a hairdresser—she owned the hairdressing salon in the High Street. She was always worrying about it, because it didn't have many customers—most people went to the big, new hairdressers, at the other end of the High Street. Mum was always trying to think of schemes to make her salon more popular, only none of them seemed to work. But Max knew she was the best hairdresser in Bumbleford. (She always cut Max's hair, and it looked excellent, as you can see.)

Max's sister was called Daisy. She
was a bit older than Max, and she made
everybody call her Elvira because she was
going through a phase.

Max was a quiet and thoughtful boy.
He liked drawing, reading, and swimming,
but most of all he liked animals. What he
wanted more than anything else in the
whole world was a pet. He would have

liked to share the top floor flat with a cat.
Better still, he would have liked a dog.
But Max's mum was too busy with her
hair salon, and Max's dad was too busy
building things. Neither of them had time
to look after a dog.

'I could look after it myself!' Max said.
'I'd get up early and feed it and take it for
a walk before I went to school, and then
it could just sleep till I came home in the
afternoon.' He showed them a chart he had
made of the Best Dogs. But Mum and Dad
didn't think it would be fair to keep a dog
in a top-floor flat.

Max tried getting his sister Daisy to
have a word with them. She was older
than Max, so he thought she might be able
to persuade them. But Daisy only liked

scary animals. 'We should get a wolf, or a vampire bat!' she said. 'Or a giant, bird-eating spider!'

'We are NOT getting a giant, bird-eating spider, Daisy!' said Dad. (He was scared of creepy-crawlies.)

'My name is not Daisy!' said Daisy. 'I am ELVIRA.' And she went back into her bedroom, slammed the door, and listened to gloomy music very loudly.

So Max had to be content with cuddly animals instead. He had quite a large collection of those, and he was very fond of all of them, but it wasn't the same as having a real, live pet. That night, as he lay in bed listening to the wild wind howl and hoo around the tall building, Max felt very sad. I *so* wish I had a pet, he thought.

It doesn't even have to be a dog or a cat, almost any sort of pet would do . . .

And then, from somewhere just outside his bedroom window, there came a loud **DOOF** and a quiet 'Bother!'

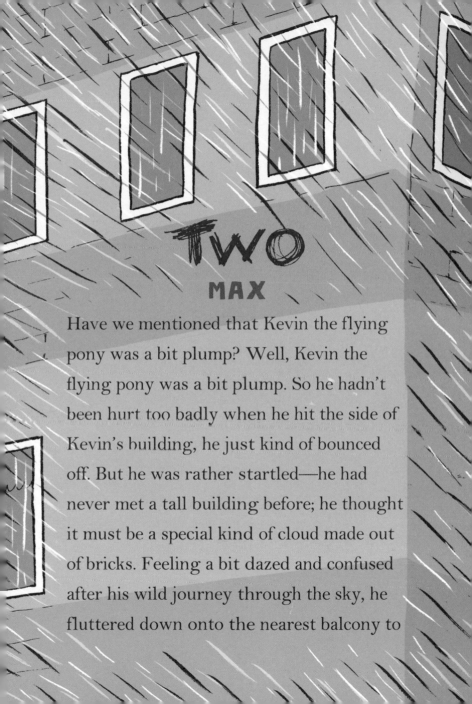

TWO

MAX

Have we mentioned that Kevin the flying pony was a bit plump? Well, Kevin the flying pony was a bit plump. So he hadn't been hurt too badly when he hit the side of Kevin's building, he just kind of bounced off. But he was rather startled—he had never met a tall building before; he thought it must be a special kind of cloud made out of bricks. Feeling a bit dazed and confused after his wild journey through the sky, he fluttered down onto the nearest balcony to have a rest. Unfortunately he landed rather awkwardly and bumped his wing.

The balcony was the balcony outside Max's bedroom. (It was the biggest bedroom in the flat, and it had been Daisy's, but she said it looked much too cheerful when the sunlight streamed in through the windows, so she let Max have it. She had moved into his old bedroom, which she had painted black.)

There wasn't any sunlight streaming in when Max opened the curtains, because it was still the middle of the night. There wasn't even any moonlight, because it was still raining hard and the sky was full of fat, black, hurrying clouds. There was only the dim orange glow of the street lights below. It was just bright enough for

Max to see that there was something
on the balcony, and that the something
was an animal. He fetched his torch, but
the battery was going so he still couldn't
tell what sort of animal it was. For a
moment Max felt a little bit afraid. It
looked like quite a big sort of animal.
What if it turned out to be a fearsome
polar bear?

Don't be silly, he told himself, how

could a fearsome polar bear have got all the way up here?

But he opened the door onto the balcony very carefully, just in case.

As soon as he stepped out onto the balcony he could see that the animal wasn't a fearsome polar bear or a fearsome anything. 'You're a pony!' he said. 'But hang on—how did a pony get all the way up here?'

Kevin flapped his little, wet, white wings. 'Ow!' he said.

'Oh!' said Max. 'You're a FLYING pony!'

He had always thought winged horses were only in stories, but here one was on his balcony, and he could see that it needed his help. It looked all shivery and sorry for itself, and it kept twitching one of its wings. Very gently Max stroked its soggy mane.

'Do you have a name, little pony?' he asked.

'Kevin,' said Kevin.

'You can talk!' said Max, who hadn't really been expecting an answer.

'Kevin,' said Kevin, nodding wisely.

'Where have you come from?' asked Max.

Kevin just neighed, very quietly. He knew a few words, but not enough to explain about the wild, wet hills of the Outermost West and the storm which had blown him out of his tree.

'Well, you're in Bumbleford now,' said Max. 'That's the name of this town. And my name is Max.' He tried stroking the pony's twitchy wing.

'Ow!' said Kevin.

'I think you've sprained it, you poor thing,' said Max. He stood and wondered what to do. He had always wanted to have an animal to look after, but now that one had arrived he wasn't quite sure what to do. He thought he should ask Mum and Dad, but it was still the middle of the night and he didn't want to wake them up. Besides, he already knew what the pony needed most. It needed to get inside, out of the cold and the wind and the rain. So he opened the door wide and the pony stood up and came clip-clopping into his bedroom.

Max fetched the towel from his Swimming Things bag and dried Kevin as best he could. Then he put his duvet over him to keep him warm.

'I expect you're hungry,' Max said. 'But I don't know what flying ponies eat. Do you eat hay, like ordinary ponies? Or do you eat seeds and worms and things, like birds?'

Kevin snorted and shook his head hard
to get rid of the idea of eating worms.
'Biscuits!' he whinnied.

'What sort?' asked Max.

'Custard creams,' said Kevin.

That was a stroke
of luck, because
custard creams were
Max's dad's favourite,
too. There was a big tin of
them in one of the cupboards in the
kitchen. Leaving Kevin to shiver under
his duvet, Max crept to his bedroom door
and let himself out. The hinges of the door
squeaked a bit, but he didn't think anyone
would hear over all the noise the wind was
making as it howled and hooed
around the outside of the flat.

He tiptoed past the room where Mum and Dad were sleeping, past Daisy's door with its **NO LITTLE BROTHERS** and **VAMPIRES WELCOME** signs, crossed the corner of the living room, and went into the kitchen. Quiet as a mouse, he opened the cupboard, opened the biscuit tin, and took out a custard cream. Then he took another one, because he thought a flying pony as fat as Kevin might be able to manage two biscuits. Then he took a third, because he thought maybe he should have one himself to keep Kevin company. (Max was very thoughtful like that.)

He was just tiptoeing back across the living room with the biscuits in his hand when a voice whispered, 'Isn't it WONDERFUL!'

THREE

A FISTFUL
OF BISCUITS

'Eeek!' said Max, but he still had
his wits about him, so he said it
very quietly. 'Daisy! What are
you doing?'

His sister was standing in front of
the big living room window, looking out
at the rain. 'Don't call me Daisy,' she
said. 'I am Elvira! But isn't the storm
WONDERFUL? Listen, how the wind
howls! What sad music it makes! And how
the torn clouds scud across the pale
face of the moon!'

Max sighed. Daisy hadn't been the same since she went on that class outing to see the Bumbleford Amateur Dramatic Society's version of *Dracula* when she was in Year Eight. Ever since, she'd been fascinated by stories about gruesome ghosts, gloomy tombs, and sad ladies in lonely towers. Mum and Dad said it was just a phase she was going through, but it had lasted nearly two whole terms now and Max thought it was high time she got over it.

'On a night like this, witches and spirits may be abroad!' she said, gesturing dramatically at the storm.

'I don't blame them,' said Max. 'I expect they've probably gone somewhere nice and sunny, like Spain.'

'Not that sort of abroad,' said Daisy. '"Abroad" means "out and about".'

'Why not just say "out and about" then?'

'Because "abroad" sounds more old-fashioned and POETIC,' said Daisy. She turned back to the window as another massive gust of wind leaned against it. 'On a night like this, who knows what strange creatures may be out and about? Vampires, and ghosts, and . . .'

'Fat flying ponies?' suggested Max, who just wished she'd shut up and let him get back to his room with Kevin's biscuits.

'Fat flying ponies?' said Daisy. 'Don't be so silly!' She gave him one of her hard stares. 'What are you doing out of bed anyway?'

'You're still up,' said Max.

'That's different. I am a creature of

the darkness, I love the moth-haunted mournfulness of midnight. You're just a little boy, and it's long past your bedtime. Have you been stealing biscuits?'

'No,' said Max, holding the three custard creams carefully out of sight behind his back.

'Hmmm,' said Daisy. She was an observant girl and Max looked exactly like a person who was hiding three stolen biscuits behind his back. (She couldn't tell they were custard creams, though—she wasn't *that* good.) 'Well, get back to bed and leave me to my sad and important thoughts, or I'll tell Mum and Dad.'

Max shrugged, and hurried off to his bedroom.

'Oooh, custard creams!' said Kevin, when he saw the biscuits in Max's hand. They were a bit squashed because Max had sort of squeezed them when Daisy made him jump, but Kevin didn't seem to mind.

He ate two, and he enjoyed them so much that Max gave him the one he had been saving for himself as well, which was very nice of him.

Kevin was still rather damp, and his wing hurt, but he was starting to feel a bit better. He decided that he liked this boy who had been so kind to him. He put his nose against Max's cheek and made a sort of snorty noise which meant 'Thank you'. It tickled a bit, and made Max laugh.

Then Max snuggled down next to Kevin, and pulled the duvet over them both. His bedroom was starting to smell quite strongly of wet pony, but there was nothing Max could do about that. In the morning he would tell Mum and Dad about his strange midnight visitor.

He fell asleep wondering what they
would think of Kevin. Would they let
him stay?

FOUR

THE FLOOD

All through the night, the rain which had
been falling on the wild, western hills had
been gurgling down the streams and little
rivers into the big River Bumble, which
ran through the middle of Bumbleford.
The river had been rising higher and
higher, and flowing faster and faster.

Just before breakfast time a trickle of water came over the riverbank, and the trickle turned into a stream, and the stream turned into a whole new river and went roaring off down the High Street, splashing and gurgling as if it was excited to be running over pavements and roads instead of a river bed. It lifted up parked cars and played with them for a bit and left them in untidy heaps. It turned the market square into a lake, and all the buildings into islands. It spilled into shops and restaurants.

All over Bumbleford, people woke up to unexpected sloshing and slopping sounds. Cats and dogs who had been asleep in people's kitchens went running upstairs to shake themselves dry and warn their owners that things were getting awfully wet downstairs. Two guinea pigs floated out of an open window, and set sail across the town in their hutch. The guinea pigs' names were Beyoncé and Neville, and they thought it was excellent fun, but nobody else did.

Bumbleford was flooded!

And the rain was still falling down and down . . .

And the water was
still rising up and up . . .

'Mum,' said Max, at
breakfast time. 'There's a fat
flying pony in my room.'
'That's nice, dear,' said Mum.
'He blew onto my balcony last
night,' said Max. 'He's hurt his
wing. His name's Kevin.'
'Really?' said Dad. But he wasn't
listening. Neither of them were. They
were watching the local news on TV.

'Shocking scenes in Bumbleford, where the whole town centre is now underwater!' said the newsreader.

'Oh no, my poor hairdressing salon,' said Max's mum.

'The local lifeboat was launched to help people trapped in their houses,' the newsreader went on, 'but unfortunately it was a non-waterproof lifeboat and it dissolved. The mayor has declared a state of emergency!'

The TV studio was flooding, too. The newsreader's desk began to float. He climbed on top of it and started using a clipboard as a paddle.

'Abandon town!' he shouted, paddling off the side of the screen. 'Women, children, and newsreaders first!'

The water rose until the TV set looked like a goldfish tank. A fish swam up to the camera and made fishy faces at it. Then the water must have got into the camera, because the screen went snowy. It must have got into Bumbleford's power station too, because the TV turned off, and all the lights went out. The hum of the fridge and the other small, steady sounds that

Max never really noticed on normal days suddenly stopped, all at once. The flat filled with a surprised silence.

'This is a pain!' said Mum. 'The town is flooded, and now we've got no electricity!'

'It's not a pain, it's a CALAMITY!' wailed Daisy, checking her phone. 'We've got no Wi-Fi! Without Wi-Fi I'll DIE!'

'Now, everyone keep calm,' said Dad.

'Yes,' said Max. 'Come and see my pony . . .'

He grabbed Mum by the hand and started pulling her away from the breakfast table, but just as they were passing the living room window they heard someone knocking on the glass.

Outside were Mr and Mrs Brown, who lived on the ground floor. They were

roped together
like mountaineers
and carrying
enormous backpacks.
Mum slid the window
open and said, 'What
on earth are you
doing out there?'

'Our flat's flooded!'

said Mr Brown, sounding quite pleased about it.

'How dreadful!' said Mum.

'Oh, we don't mind!' said Mrs Brown. 'We like adventures. Usually we have to go hiking in the hills to find them, but now an adventure has come knocking at our own front door . . .'

'Well, more sort of trickling underneath it,' said Mr Brown.

'The water was a metre deep and rising fast when we woke up,' Mrs Brown went on. 'So I said to Nigel, "Nigel," I said, "you know what this is? It's a flood!" So we packed our survival gear and some essential supplies and we headed for the high ground. That's you; your flat is the highest place in the whole town.

You don't mind if we stay?'

They came into the room, dripping on the carpet and coiling up their climbing ropes.

'You climbed up the side of the building?' asked Dad, coming to help them off with their backpacks.

'Yes!' said Mr Brown. 'You mustn't use the stairs in a flood, that's very important.'

'I think you're thinking of lifts and fires,' said Mum. 'You're not supposed to use lifts in a fire.'

'Stairs in a flood can be just as dangerous,' said Mrs Brown firmly. (The truth was, they had just been happy to have an excuse to use their mountaineering skills and all their climbing gear.)

After that it was useless trying to make Mum and Dad understand about Kevin; they were too busy making cups of tea on the Browns' camping stove and talking about the flood. So Max helped himself to some more custard creams and went back to his room to see how Kevin was.

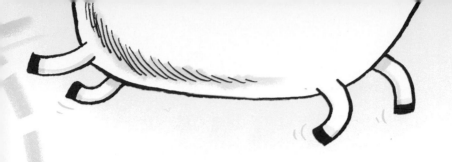

FIVE

ON THE ROOF

Kevin was happy enough. His sprained wing was feeling much better and he was trying it out by flying round and round Max's bedroom. Max had to duck to avoid his hooves as he went by. When he noticed Max watching he landed just in front of him, and looked at him in a way that Max knew meant he wanted Max to climb on his back and have a ride.

'Are you sure?' asked Max. 'You're quite a small pony, and you have hurt your wing . . .'

But Kevin just nodded, so Max jumped
up on his bed and from there onto Kevin's
wide, white back.

Kevin was surprisingly strong. His little wings flapped so fast they were just a blur, and he rose off the floor with Max clinging to his mane. It was a bit scary at first, but Max hung on tight and soon learned how to keep his balance as Kevin circled the room. 'Ha ha!' he laughed. Kevin was having a good time, too. He'd been missing his home in the wild, wet hills and his own nice comfy nest, but when Max was around he didn't mind the missing so much. He had never really thought about it before, but being the only fat flying pony in the hills got a bit lonely sometimes. It was a nice change having someone to play with.

Faster and faster they flew. The draught from Kevin's wings dragged

posters off the walls, and one of
his hooves knocked an avalanche
of books off Max's shelves. Then
Max's head hit the lampshade. It
didn't hurt, because the lampshade
was one of those big paper ones,
but the shade came loose and went
crashing to the floor.

'Oops,' said Kevin.

He settled on the end of the bed and ate the custard creams while Max looked about at the wreckage. It was starting to seem to him as if a bedroom might not be the best place to keep a flying pony. It wasn't just the books and the posters and the lampshade—there were muddy little hoofprints all over the carpet, and white pony hair on the duvet.

And was that pony poo in the waste paper basket?

Max opened the curtains and looked out onto the balcony. It had stopped raining now, but the balcony still looked a bit of a cheerless place for a pony to be. He was worried that if he made Kevin stay out there he

might get bored and fly away. Then he
had an idea.

'Come on, Kevin!' he said.

He opened his bedroom door, and
the pony followed him out into the hall.
The grown-ups were still in the living
room, talking seriously about the flood.
None of them even looked up as Max led
Kevin past. He opened the front door,
and they went out together onto the
landing.

Even though Max's flat was on the
top floor, there was still a flight of stairs
outside it that led up to another door. This
door opened onto the roof of the building.
It was locked mostly, but Gordon who
lived on the second floor kept his pigeons
in a coop on the roof, and sometimes when

he was away he asked Max to go up and
feed them, so Max had a key.

He opened the door, and Kevin went
out onto the roof, sniffing interestedly at
the cool, rain-smelling air. The roof was
big and flat, with a rail around the edge to
stop people falling off. There were some
satellite dishes there, and some aerials,

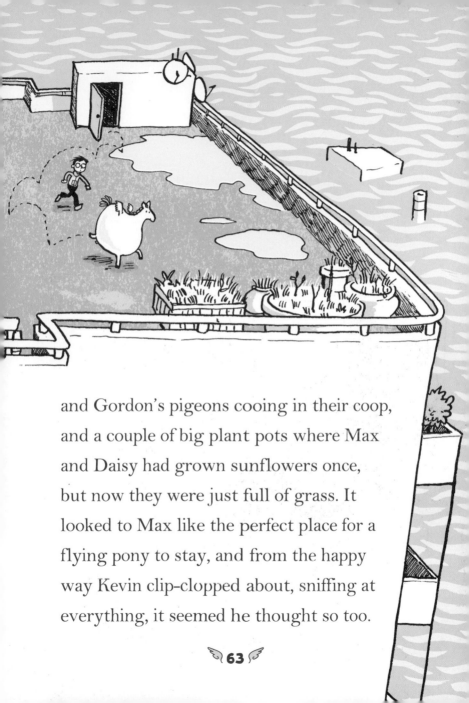

and Gordon's pigeons cooing in their coop,
and a couple of big plant pots where Max
and Daisy had grown sunflowers once,
but now they were just full of grass. It
looked to Max like the perfect place for a
flying pony to stay, and from the happy
way Kevin clip-clopped about, sniffing at
everything, it seemed he thought so too.

Max went to the edge of the roof and stood on tiptoe so he could peer over the rail. He was startled to see how high the water had risen. The familiar streets he usually looked down on had turned into a maze of canals.

People were rowing about down there in inflatable dinghies. This is awful, thought Max. Everyone's stuff will be ruined! And how much further is the water going to rise?

Behind him, Kevin ate the grass in the sunflower pots, and burped. 'Custard creams?' he said hopefully. He was a hungry pony, and his long flight through the storm had given him an extra-big appetite.

'I'll get you some,' said Max. 'Wait here . . .'

But when he let himself back into the flat, he found that more visitors had arrived while he had been up on the roof. Gordon from the second floor and Tiffany Binns from the flat underneath Max's had come upstairs to shelter too.

'The water is waist-deep in my flat!' said Gordon, as a pigeon popped out of his pocket.

'We're all going to be washed away!' twittered Tiffany Binns.

'Nonsense,' said Max's mum. 'The rain's stopped. The flood must start going down soon.

'I don't know about that,' said Gordon, who was quite old and had probably seen a few floods in his time. 'This isn't just an ordinary flood, you know. That storm last night blew in from the Outermost West, and that's a very strange place. All sorts of creatures live out there that most people don't even believe in any more. Magical things like mermaids and monsters. It stands to reason that weather from a place like that might be a bit magical too.'

'What about flying ponies?' asked Max. 'Do flying ponies live in the Outermost West?'

Gordon nodded. 'Why, yes; I believe I have heard stories of flying ponies making their nests in the wild woods there.'

Max went into the kitchen. Mr and
Mrs Brown were busy cooking something
horrible-smelling on their camp stove.
Daisy was eating biscuits. Max grabbed
the tin from her.

It was empty!

'You've eaten all the custard creams!' he yelled.

'You mean *you've* eaten them all!' said Daisy. 'There were only four left.'

Max went and looked in the cupboard. There were no packets of custard creams there. There were no biscuits at all.

'We're running out of food,' said Daisy. 'All these visitors are eating it all, and there wasn't much to start with because Mum was going to go to the shops today. But she can't go now, because the shops are underwater. We'll probably have to starve.'

'No we won't!' said Mrs Brown cheerfully, taking a saucepan off her camping stove and tipping some brown stuff with bits in it into a bowl. 'Look! Emergency rations! Me and Nigel lived on these when we were hiking across Scotland. They come as powder in a packet and you just add hot water to turn them into a lovely meal.'

'They also make good wallpaper paste,' said Mr Brown.

'Try some!' said Mrs Brown.

Max took the bowl from her and sniffed it suspiciously. 'What is it meant to be?' he asked.

Mr Brown looked at the packet the stuff had come in. 'It says, "Brown Stuff With Bits In It",' he said.

'Are there any other flavours?' Max asked.

Mrs Brown waved another packet. 'This one is Brown Stuff Without Bits In It! Mmm! Scrummy!'

'Thank you, but I'm not really hungry,' said Max, and passed the bowl to Daisy. Then he hurried out of the kitchen. He didn't fancy brown stuff, with or without bits in it, and he felt sure that it wouldn't be the sort of thing fat flying ponies liked. He had to find more biscuits!

He went to the hall cupboard and rummaged around among the shoes and coats until he found the diving mask and flippers he'd learned to use when he was on holiday at Farsight Cove last summer. Then he fetched his swimming trunks, and a towel, and two big shopping bags, and some string, and ran back up to the roof, where Kevin was checking the flowerpots again to see if there were any bits of grass he had missed.

'Kevin,' he said, 'I need your help.'

Kevin thought about it. Nobody had ever asked him for help before, and he wasn't sure he would be any good at it.

'There are no biscuits left,' said Max. 'We can get more, but we're going to have to work together. It might be dangerous, but we'll be OK, because we'll look after each other. Because we're friends, and that's what friends do.'

Kevin had never had a friend before, either. There were other magical creatures who he bumped into from time to time in the wild, wet hills, and the hikers who had shared their biscuits with him, but none of them had really been a friend. He thought about it, and decided that he liked the idea. So he gave Max's face a big, wet lick, to show that he was ready to help.

'Great!' said Max. As quickly as he could, he took off all his clothes.

Coo! said the pigeons in Gordon's coop.

Max pulled on his swimming trunks, flippers and mask. He wrapped the towel around Kevin's neck like a scarf. He tied the shopping bags to each other with a long loop of string and hung them over Kevin's wide back so they dangled down on either side, like panniers. Then he climbed up and sat between them.

'Come on!' he said. 'Let's go shopping!'

FLAP

FLAP

FLAP

FLAP

FLAP

SIX

KEVIN GOES SHOPPING

Kevin galloped toward the edge of the
roof, flapping his wings as fast they would
go. The pigeons watched enviously as he
jumped over the railing and soared into
the sky. Then they all ducked as he came
swooping back right over their coop.
Kevin had never flown in a town before,
and it was very exciting. He whirled
around the outside of Max's flat and
went diving down until his hooves almost

FLAP

touched the water. He nearly collided with
a pair of guinea pigs who had made a sail
for their hutch from a plastic bag and were
steering towards the park. But he pulled
up just in time, and went flapping off up
the flooded High Street.

Max held on tight to the towel he had
tied around Kevin's neck, and waved to
everyone they passed. Some people were
paddling about on airbeds and canoes;
others were camped out on the rooftops

or watching from high windows. Max had expected them to be amazed when they saw a boy on a fat white pony go flying past, but they didn't seem too surprised.

He soon found out why. There was a whole list of surprising things to see in Bumbleford that morning, and fat flying ponies didn't even make the top three. Gordon had been right about the storm. It had woken up all sorts of strange creatures who don't usually come near the places where ordinary people live.

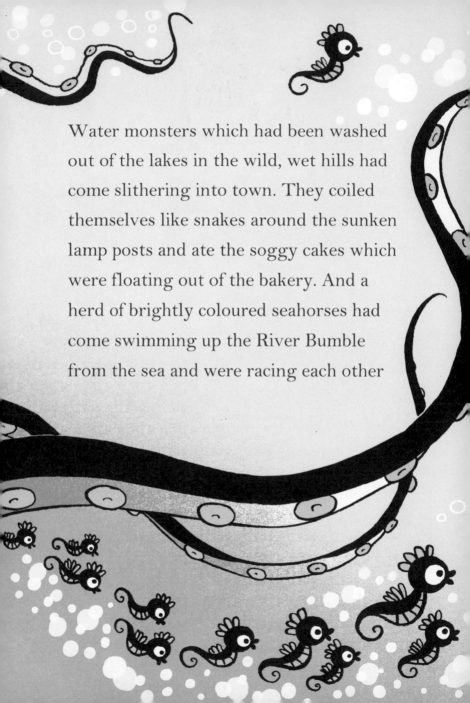

Water monsters which had been washed
out of the lakes in the wild, wet hills had
come slithering into town. They coiled
themselves like snakes around the sunken
lamp posts and ate the soggy cakes which
were floating out of the bakery. And a
herd of brightly coloured seahorses had
come swimming up the River Bumble
from the sea and were racing each other

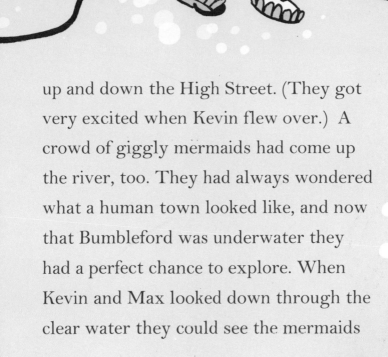

up and down the High Street. (They got very excited when Kevin flew over.) A crowd of giggly mermaids had come up the river, too. They had always wondered what a human town looked like, and now that Bumbleford was underwater they had a perfect chance to explore. When Kevin and Max looked down through the clear water they could see the mermaids

swimming in and out of the flooded shops,
helping themselves to clothes and shoes.
(They didn't have any feet to wear the
shoes on, of course; they just put them on
their heads, like hats.) A giant octopus
had found its way into the shoe shop
too. It was trying on four pairs of
trendy trainers.

Kevin landed on top of the
clocktower near the supermarket
and folded his wings.

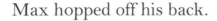

Max hopped off his back.

'Stay here!' he said. 'I'll be back in a minute.'

'Custard creams!' said Kevin happily.

Max scrambled down the clock face, took a deep breath, and jumped off the number six into the waves.

It was very strange to be underwater, swimming past all the familiar shops. The sunlight came down in silvery fingers through the wave tops and tickled the shop signs. Max peered in through the window of his mum's hairdressing salon. It was usually very quiet, because most people had their hair done at the bigger salons at the other end of the High Street. Mum worried about it—she was always saying that if she didn't start getting more customers soon,

the salon might have to close down.
Max wished she could see it today.
Although it was full of water, it was also
full of mermaids. They were milling about
inside, admiring all the photographs of
fancy hairstyles, which were pinned up
on the walls. Some were putting curlers
in their hair, and opening bottles of dye
which made huge clouds in the water like
multi-coloured squid ink. A few saw Max
looking in at them, and waved.

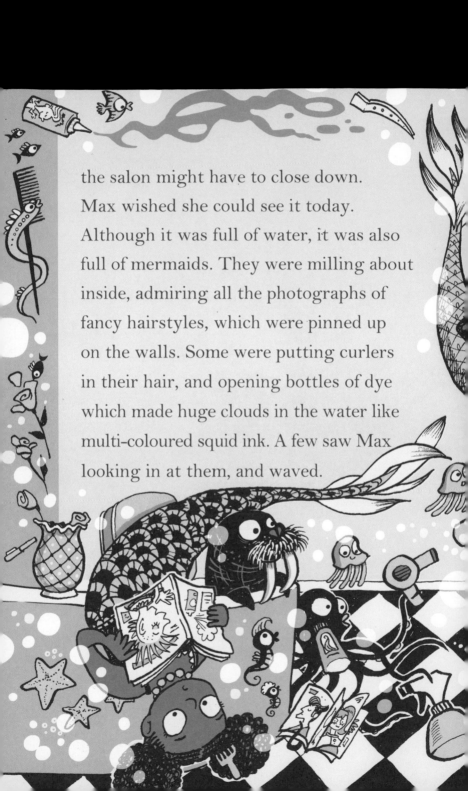

Max had been staring at them for so long that he had run out of air. He swam back to the surface, took another huge gulp, and dived down again, aiming for the supermarket.

The supermarket was surprisingly busy, too. Quite a lot of people had been caught, like Max's family, without much food in the house when the flood arrived, so those who owned snorkels or aqualungs were fetching supplies for the rest. Mrs Oliveira the supermarket manager stood at the door in her diving suit, holding a board where she'd written in waterproof ink, **EVERYTHING FREE TODAY**. That was a stroke of luck, thought Max, because he'd completely forgotten to bring any money with him.

The second big breath he had taken
before he jumped off the clock was
already starting to run out, and bits of it
kept escaping in silver bubbles from the
corners of his mouth, so he grabbed a
basket from the pile beside Mrs Oliveira
and swam quickly along the aisles to the
biscuit section.

(He knew his way because the biscuit section was the best bit of the supermarket.) Lots of mermaids were gathered there, opening packets of biscuits and trying them, but they were mostly going for the chocolate ones, and lots of packets of Kevin's favourites were floating about untouched. Max gathered them up and wedged them into his basket. He was getting ready to leave when he noticed a twin pack of custard creams, just behind a hungry mermaid.

'Excuse me,' he said without thinking, as he reached for it. But that was a mistake, because the last of the breath he had been holding came out with the words, and water rushed in. Snatching the biscuits in one hand and towing his full basket with the other he swam out of the shop and kicked his way back to the surface.

'I did it!' he shouted, as he climbed back onto the clocktower roof. He started taking packets of biscuits out of the basket and putting them into the shopping bags, ready to hang them over Kevin's back. He thought how pleased Mum and Dad would be with him when he went home with fresh supplies. Then he wondered what they'd say when the fresh supplies turned out to be just biscuits. 'I'm going to have to go back down,' he told to Kevin. 'Mum says we need a balanced diet.'

Kevin was a bit confused by that, because he thought biscuits and then more biscuits was a very balanced diet. But he nodded very wisely, as if he understood, and watched while Max took another huge, deep breath and dived again.

Max swam through the supermarket grabbing apples, bananas, tins of beans,

and a big bag of frozen broccoli. The fresh
bread had all been ruined by the water, but
he found some sliced loaves in bags which
looked waterproof. A huge plastic bottle with

oranges on the label drifted by and he grabbed that too, because he liked orange juice.

Outside in the warm sunshine, Kevin was exploring the clocktower roof. There were sculptures of a lion and unicorn on the very top and he was a bit scared of them at first, until he worked out that they weren't real. He went and stood beside them. He tried to copy the lion's brave pose, and he made faces at the unicorn. (Kevin had met unicorns before, and they'd all been horrid show-offs.)

When he looked down at the
supermarket again he saw Max pop to the
surface with another basket full of food.
He gave a welcoming sort of whinny and
made ready to flap down and say hello,
but just then he noticed something else.

Zooming through the water towards
Max was something dark. Something with
a black, triangular fin.

A shark!

Kevin had never actually seen a shark,
but he had heard about them. They had
always sounded really scary, with their
big pointy teeth and their big black fins
and their slimy tentacles. Or was that
octopuses? But whatever, he didn't want a

horrible shark eating his friend!

Brave as any lion, Kevin launched himself off the top of the clocktower and dived towards the oncoming shark. It was a really big one, and he was a bit frightened of it, but he made himself keep going. 'Leave Max alone!' he whinnied, and crash-landed on top of the fearsome fish when it was just a few metres from Max.

SPLASH! The shark came to pieces, and all the pieces swam off in different directions, laughing madly. It turned out it wasn't a shark at all. It was a load of naughty little web-footed monkeys who had been swimming along in a clump, holding a cardboard cut-out fin to make people think they were a shark.

They were Sea Monkeys: smelly,
shouty, mischievous little creatures who
hatched out of the seaweed which washed up
on the shores of the Outermost West. They
usually lived in big gangs on the rocky
beaches there, but now they had decided
to come and have some fun in Bumbleford.
They scrambled onto nearby buildings
or the tops of lamp posts and jeered at
Kevin. One tried to steal the basket of food
which Max had just brought up from the
supermarket, but Kevin wasn't having that.
He took off, shook himself dry in mid-air,
and swooped low over the water so
that Max could grab his hooves as
he went by. He carried Max and the
basket up to the top of the clock tower,
and Max draped the shopping bags

back over Kevin, filled them and towelled himself dry.

Max had been planning to swim back down and return the baskets to the pile outside the supermarket, but it did not seem like a good idea with all those naughty monkeys around, so he just stacked them one inside the other and dropped them off the clocktower, hoping that they would sink down to roughly the right place. Then he slung the bag over Kevin's back and they started to fly home.

They were both feeling happy and triumphant. Max was looking forward to telling his parents and the neighbours about his adventures underwater and all the strange visitors the flood had brought to Bumbleford. One of the loaves he had found turned out to be all soggy inside its bag, and the orange juice wasn't orange juice at all, it was super-concentrated fruity-fresh bubble bath, but he still knew Mum and Dad would be pleased.

As for Kevin, he was mostly looking forward to the biscuits. But he knew that he had been terribly brave in saving Max from the shark, even if it had turned out to be only Sea Monkeys. He had *thought* it was a shark, and that was what counted. He decided that he should award himself a medal, but he wasn't sure where you got medals from, so he decided to award himself some extra biscuits instead.

They were just flying over Max's school when they heard a voice below them shouting 'Help!'

SEVEN
MONKEY BUSINESS

Mr Mould, the head teacher, was sitting on the last little bit of the school roof, which stuck up out of the water. Like Max he was wearing a diving mask and flippers, but of course he wasn't in his swimming trunks—that would have been far too undignified. He was wearing his usual suit and tie, and he was very wet.

Kevin swooped lower, and Max saw that the water around Mr Mould's perch was full of Sea Monkeys. They were blowing raspberries and pulling faces at the head teacher, and some of them were throwing things.

EEP!

'Help!' said Mr Mould again,
as a well-aimed whiteboard
rubber bounced off his head.

Poor Mr Mould. He didn't think anyone had an excuse to take a day off school just because school happened to be underwater, so he had put on his flippers and turned up for work as normal that morning. But when he got there, he found that the school had been invaded by Sea Monkeys.

The mischievous creatures were having a great time pretending to be children, and they were making even more of a noise and a mess than real ones. When Mr Mould arrived the monkeys all clustered round him, making faces and blowing underwater raspberries. 'Now you cut that out, you horrible little . . .' said Mr Mould.

But, horrible little what? When kids misbehaved he called them 'horrible little monkeys', but the Sea Monkeys were monkeys already, so it probably wouldn't be much of an insult. While he was still trying to think of what to call them, the monkeys rushed at him, and he had to swim as fast he could back to the surface. That was how he came to be perching on the roof while the monkeys swam around below him, hooting with laughter and making rude remarks about his flippers. He had been up there all morning. Once, a sort of boat had gone by, and he had shouted to it to come and help him, but it turned out to be just two guinea pigs on a floating hutch and they had sailed right past.

Just when he was thinking that he might have to swim home through a whole shoal of cheeky monkeys, he saw the plump white shape of Kevin come flapping overhead.

'Help!' he shouted. 'Help! Help!'

Now, some children might not bother rescuing their head teacher from Sea Monkeys. Some children might think that being stuck on a school roof surrounded by floodwaters and marauding monkeys is a pretty good place for a head teacher to be, and that the best thing would be just to leave them there and pretend you hadn't heard their cries for help. But Max was not that sort of child. He only had to think about it for a short time before he decided that he was going to have to try and rescue Mr Mould.

Kevin flew down towards the roof, but the monkeys just thought that added to the fun. They started throwing things at Kevin too. The poor pony flinched as soggy maths textbooks and plastic trays from the school canteen whizzed past his nose like frisbees.

HEY KIDS! LET'S LEARN MATHS!

EEP! EEP! EEP! EEP! EEP! EEP! EEP! EEP! EEP! EEP! EEP! EEP!

Max almost slipped off his back.

Kevin flew higher. 'Too many monkeys!' he whinnied.

But Max had an idea. He rummaged among the shopping and pulled out the bag of frozen broccoli. He thought those frozen florets would be just the thing to scare Sea Monkeys away. He ripped the bag open with his teeth and told Kevin to fly down low again. As the pony went swooping over the water towards Mr Mould and the Sea Monkeys, he shouted, 'Bombs away!' and tipped out the

broccoli. The hard green blobs of frozen
veg made white splashes all around the
Sea Monkeys, and hit quite a few of them.

They shrieked with surprise, but they
didn't scatter or dive back underwater
as Max had hoped. They stayed on the
surface in a big clump, shouting and
giggling at Max. '**EEP!** Missed us!'
they squealed. 'You're rubbish!'

'You smell!' Max yelled back. It was
a bit of a rude thing to say, but it was
true—even from up in the sky, on Kevin's

EEP!

EEP!

EEP! EEP! EEP!

back, he could smell the grubby little monkeys. They smelled like his P.E. socks, only worse. They smelled like boiled Brussels sprouts and damp towels and school toilets. 'You stink!' Max yelled.

But the monkeys just laughed. **'EEP! EEP! EEP!'**

'They like being being stinky! ' said Kevin. 'They're Sea Monkeys!'

That gave Max another idea. 'Fly back down,' he said. And as Kevin turned in mid-air and

EEF

swooped back over the school roof, he unscrewed the cap on the fruity-fresh bubble-bath bottle and upended it.

GLOOP! All the liquid poured out. It splashed over the monkeys and spilled into the water all around them. '**ACK! ICK! URGH!**' they said, looking at one another in confusion. They sniffed at the stuff that covered them. They didn't like its fruity-fresh smell one bit. (They didn't know it was bubble bath. The whole idea of baths was new to them.)

EEP?

'Quick!' said Max, 'Zwoosh it up!'

Kevin belly-flopped into the water and started swimming round and round the monkeys, with his little legs churning the water like egg-beaters. The monkeys yelled and swam towards him, but before they

could reach him he was hidden by a great wall of bubbles. The monkeys squealed and chittered. They flapped about in the water, trying to brush the bubbles off, but that just made more bubbles. 'Eep!' they wailed. 'Argh! We're all clean!'

Kevin took off again. He soared over the struggling, bubbling monkeys and hovered just above the school roof while Mr Mould climbed onto his back behind Max. 'Thank you, Max!' the head teacher spluttered. 'I'll let you off homework for a whole week for this!'

Kevin flew lower and more slowly now that he had a whole head teacher to carry as well as Max and the shopping, but the monkeys were hidden in a cloud of bubbles and didn't see him. By the time they fought their way out, furious and fruity-fresh, Kevin was just a tiny dot in the distance, flying home towards Max's flat.

The monkeys threw a few pencil sharpeners and things after him, just to make themselves feel better. Then they

went back underwater and started
writing rude words on the school walls,
and they didn't even spell them properly
or bother to use capital letters and full
stops; it was an absolute disgrace.

FLAP FLAP FLAP FLAP

EIGHT

KEVIN TO THE RESCUE

By the time Kevin and Max got home
the flat was getting quite crowded. Not
only were all the neighbours from the
downstairs flats camping out in Max's
living room, neighbours from other parts
of the town had arrived too, mooring their
rafts and dinghies to the balconies on the
floor below and climbing up ropes which
Mr and Mrs Brown let down for them.
Poppy, who worked with Mum at the

hair salon, was there, and some of Daisy's friends, and also a little girl called Ellie Fidgett who was upset because her guinea pigs had floated away. (Little did she know that Neville and Beyoncé had sailed safely to dry land. Their floating hutch had come ashore on a little green island where there

were plenty of interesting things to eat.
'We shall call this new country Guinea
Piggia,' squeaked Beyoncé, and Neville
made a flag out of a cocktail stick and a
sweet wrapper so that they could claim it
for all guinea-pig kind.)

Everyone stared in amazement when Kevin arrived. He circled the flat with Max and Mr Mould waving from his back. Then Max's dad opened the big balcony windows in the living room and Kevin flew inside and touched down neatly on the rug.

'Max!' said Mum. 'I thought you were in your room!'

'I've been shopping,' said Max, handing over the bags of food and biscuits. 'Oh, and we rescued Mr Mould.'

'I was being attacked by Sea Monkeys!' explained Mr Mould. 'Dreadful creatures! Dirty and dangerous and terrible at spelling! The authorities must do something!'

But everyone else was more interested in Kevin than in Mr Mould's complaints. 'Max,' said Dad, 'have my eyes gone funny or is that a fat flying pony?'

'His name's Kevin,' Max said proudly.
'He blew into my window last night in the
big storm. Can he stay with us? He can
live on the roof, and he eats biscuits.'

'Biscuits!' agreed Kevin.

'Well, I'm not sure . . .' Dad
started to say.

'Listen!' said Daisy, interrupting.

Through the open windows came
the sound of voices. 'Help!' they were
shouting. 'Max! Help!'

Everyone crowded out onto the
balcony. Below them, the rooftops of
Bumbleford were crowded with people.
The flood had risen even higher, and
now everyone was scrambling onto their
roofs to escape from the water and the

mischievous Sea Monkeys. They had seen Kevin fly over with Max and Mr Mould on his back, and they were hoping that he could airlift them to safety, too.

'It looks as if you have work to do, Max,' said Daisy.

'But you'd better put some warmer clothes on,' said Mum, who had noticed that Max was starting to shiver a bit in his wet trunks.

So he did. While he was getting dressed, Daisy fed Kevin a whole packet of custard creams. Then Max climbed onto Kevin's back again and they took off from the balcony and began their daring mission.

To and fro they went, ferrying people from the roofs of their submerged houses

back to Max's flat. Quite soon the flat
was full, so Kevin started lifting people to
the roof instead. Some of the people had
saved bags of food from their houses, so
Mr and Mrs Brown got their camping
stove working again and started cooking
a huge, strange meal for everybody,
made up of all the ingredients which had
been salvaged from the flood. When the
mermaids saw what was happening they

started to help, swimming to the surface
with pizzas and cakes they'd rescued from
the flooded shops. A lot of the stuff they
brought up was too soggy to use, but some
of it dried out all right.

The Sea Monkeys were no help at all, of course. They threw things at Kevin each time he flew overhead, and scrambled onto rooftops to shout, 'You're too fat to fly!' and 'Look at your silly little wings!'

Max and Kevin just ignored them— that's sometimes the best thing to do with Sea Monkeys.

The last person to be rescued was the mayor, who was sitting sadly on top of the flagpole on the roof of the town hall. 'Max, I am so glad of you and your flying pony,' she said, as she climbed onto Kevin's back. 'I had called for a helicopter to come and pick everyone up, but those awful Sea Monkeys got to the rescue station before it could take off. They took the helicopter to pieces to see how it

worked, and now it's just a big pile of parts. If it wasn't for Kevin we'd all be spending the night on our rooftops . . .'

But Kevin was growing tired. He had carried so many people up to the roof of Max's flat that he could barely flap hard enough to stay in the air. He flew lower and lower until his tummy was almost brushing the tops of the waves. Just as he was getting ready to make a last effort and fly up to the flat a cheeky Sea Monkey reached up out of the water and grabbed him by his right back hoof!

EEP!

EEP?

Kevin whinnied, and flapped himself higher, pulling the monkey out of the water. But another monkey grabbed it by the tail, and a third monkey grabbed that monkey by the tail, and pretty soon a whole chain of monkeys was dangling from Kevin's hoof, trying to drag him down into the water.

'Keep going, Kevin!' shouted Max. 'You can do it!'

Kevin strained, but the bottom-most monkey grabbed hold of the hour hand on the clocktower clock and held on tight. The mayor took off her gold chain of office and dropped it into the flood to lighten Kevin's load. He flapped harder and harder, and the Sea Monkeys squeaked and eeped and giggled with glee. Tethered to the clocktower, Kevin sank lower and lower. Worried mermaids looked up out of the water. 'Help!' Max shouted down to them.

The mermaids all vanished, diving down into the depths, away from the chain of sniggering monkeys. But then one mermaid popped up again. She was

holding something which she had taken
from the supermarket, and she reached up
and handed it to Max. Max looked at it. It
was a pot of pepper.

'What are we meant to do with pepper?'
said the mayor. 'We need to get rid of these
Sea Monkeys, not season them!'

But the mermaid had gone to join
her friends.

Once again, Max had an idea. 'Fly higher!' he told Kevin.

Kevin flapped his wings a little faster, but he was still sinking. His hooves touched the water.

'Think of the biscuits!' Max told him. 'There's a whole bag of biscuits waiting for you back at the flat!'

Kevin rose a centimetre or two.

'Bourbons!' said Max.

Kevin flapped harder.

'Pink wafers!'

Kevin flapped harder still. He was a whole metre above the water now.

'CUSTARD CREAMS!' yelled Max.

Kevin flapped as hard as he could, and rose high into the air. It was the monkeys' turn to strain now as they all

EEP!

clung tight to each other's
tails, trying to keep him
tethered to the clocktower.
But Max unscrewed the lid
of the pepper pot and emptied
it over the monkey who was
clinging to Kevin's hoof.

'**AHHH-CHOO!**' went the monkey. He still managed to hold on to Kevin's hoof, but the sneeze blew pepper powder over the next monkey in the line. '**AHHH-CHOO!**' sneezed the second monkey, and the pepper and the sneezing spread down the whole chain of monkeys—

'**AHHH-CHOO!**
AHH-CHOO!
AHHH-CHOO!'

—until the one at the very bottom sneezed so loudly that he let go of the clock.

The chain of monkeys pinged like an elastic band, shooting high into the air. They let go of each other's tails and scattered all across the town, bouncing off rooftops like hairy tennis balls, and vanishing into the floodwaters with white splashes.

Kevin whinnied in triumph, Max
and the mayor cheered, and they
flew happily back to the flat, where
everyone was waiting to welcome them.

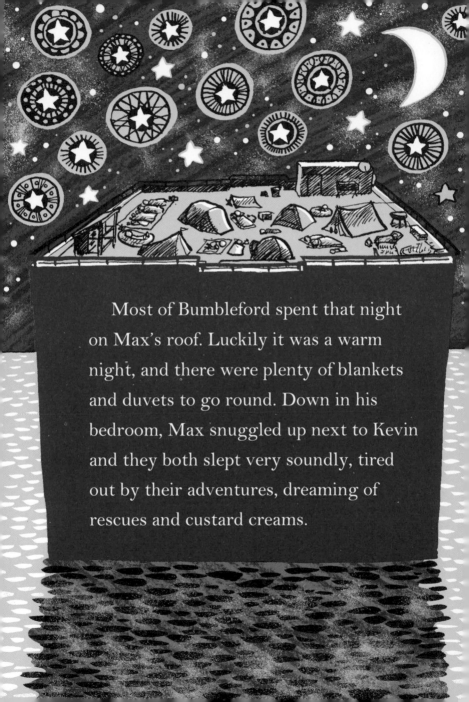

Most of Bumbleford spent that night on Max's roof. Luckily it was a warm night, and there were plenty of blankets and duvets to go round. Down in his bedroom, Max snuggled up next to Kevin and they both slept very soundly, tired out by their adventures, dreaming of rescues and custard creams.

And when they woke the next morning, and went out onto the balcony to look at the flooded town, they found that something amazing had happened. The great Bumbleford flood, which had risen so quickly, had drained away just as fast. The mermaids and other strange creatures had gone with it, back to their lakes and their homes in the ocean deeps. It was almost as if the whole thing had been a dream, except that the wet streets shone and steamed in the rising sun, and all the shops and houses were covered in starfish, like gold stickers for good behaviour, and every lamp post was festooned with seaweed streamers.

NINE
KEVIN FLIES HOME

The flood left everyone with loads of clearing up to do. Even Max's family, who had not been flooded themselves, were busy helping their neighbours. But it turned out that the mermaids had been very honest about paying for all the stuff they had taken while the shops were underwater. On the morning after the flood Max's mum and all the other shopkeepers found that their tills were stuffed with money. And it wasn't just the usual sort of money. The mermaids had taken it from the treasure chests they'd found in shipwrecks way down on the ocean floor. There were rare gold coins and precious stones and bits of antique jewellery, and it was worth so much that it paid for all the repairs and redecorating.

Quite soon, all the shops were back to normal, with one exception. Mum's hairdressing salon had been such a big hit with the mermaids that she asked Dad to waterproof it and fill it with water again.

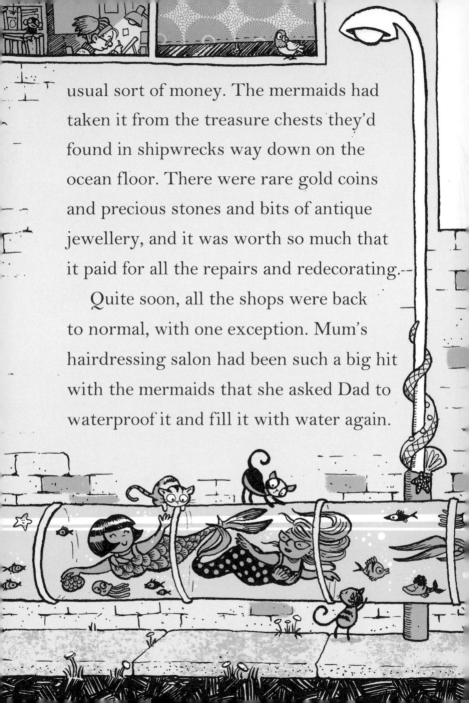

By the time he finished, it looked like a great big fish tank, and there was a pipe leading into the river so that mermaids could swim in whenever they needed a trim or a new hairdo. Mum soon got used to putting on her diving suit each morning before she went to work, and everyone in Bumbleford liked to peek in through the window when they passed and watch her and Poppy at work.

Max was worried at first that the Sea Monkeys would stay behind and make trouble, but when the water drained away all the Sea Monkeys were gone. Oddly enough, Mr and Mrs Brown's camper van was also missing, stolen from their parking space outside the flats. So if you should ever happen to see a rusty old camper van that looks as if it's full of water, and if there are little grinning faces at all the windows and a lot of giggling coming from inside, it's probably best to stay well away from it . . .

And as for Beyoncé and Neville, the brave guinea-pig explorers, when the water level dropped it turned out that their new land of Guinea Piggea was just the top of the park-keeper's compost heap. Ellie Fidgett found them there on the morning after the flood. She took them home, where they started writing a book about their adventures.

Max and his school friends had a brilliant time during the big clean-up. They went round with spatulas, carefully peeling left-behind starfish off the shop windows and plopping them into buckets of seawater. Then they took turns riding to the beach on Kevin and putting the starfish safely back in the sea.

Everyone was so grateful to Kevin and
Max for their hard work during the
flood that the mayor gave them each
a medal. She also said it would
be all right for Kevin to live
on Max's roof if he wanted
to, so he did. Dad put some
new plant pots up there and
planted grass in them, and Max
made sure his friend had a steady supply
of biscuits—not just bourbons, custard
creams and pink wafers, but also ginger
nuts and chocolate digestives and those
round ones with the bright red blob of jam
in the middle.

But at last there came the sad day when
the school was ready to reopen, and a
school is no place for a flying pony. Each

morning Max had to say goodbye to Kevin and go off to do his lessons. He did his best to concentrate all day at school, but the only thing he could think about was getting home to Kevin and going for a quick fly around the town before it got too dark.

One evening, when he went up to the roof after school, he found Kevin standing near the railing, looking out at the sunset. His tail was drooping, his ears were drooping, and he looked like a very sad pony. Gordon, who had come up to feed his pigeons, said, 'That pony is pining for his own home.'

'But this is Kevin's home!' said Max. 'He lives here now, with me!'

'He's a creature of the winds and the wild, wet hills,' said Gordon. 'Maybe he doesn't want to live in a town. Maybe it's time you helped him find his way back to where he really belongs.'

Max went and stood beside Kevin, and together they watched the sun go down. Somewhere in those evening hills must be the place where Kevin came from, Max thought. Somewhere up there he had a nest, and maybe friends he was missing.

'Do you want to go back there?' he asked. 'Do you want to go home?'

'Home!' agreed Kevin.

Max wanted to say, 'You mustn't go!' He wanted to say, 'I'll miss you so much!' But he thought Gordon was probably right. It wasn't fair to keep a magical creature like Kevin on the roof of a tower block. However much it hurt—and Max knew it was going to hurt a lot—he had to let Kevin go.

'You could just fly there, couldn't you?' he asked, trying not to let his voice go wobbly.

'Don't know where,' said Kevin, and shrugged his wings. When the storm plucked him out of his nest he had been too busy flying to pay much attention to where the wind was blowing him. The wild, wet hills of the Outermost West were a big place, and he had no idea how to find his way back to his own nest. Also, he knew he would miss all his new friends in Bumbleford, and especially Max. But the autumn winds were calling to him, and he did SO want to see his own tree again, and sniff all the familiar smells of the high hills and the open moors.

Max turned away for a moment and wiped his eyes. Then he turned back to Kevin and took a deep breath.

'I'll take you home,' he promised.

And he went very sadly back downstairs and told Mum and Dad and Daisy what they had to do.

ᵕ U ᵕ

The next weekend they all got into the car, and Dad drove west. Kevin flew above them most of the way, except sometimes he sat on the roof rack to rest his wings. Along the big roads they went, and then the middle-sized roads, and at last they

were on tiny bendy roads like tarmac
ribbons, which grew steeper and steeper
as the car wiggled its way up into the
wild, wet hills.

The air was cleaner there, and the wind was full of the smell of the moors and the wild western sea beyond. Kevin took off and soared, spreading his wings and circling higher and higher until he could see the hills laid out below him like a map. He couldn't see his nest, though, so he came back down and had a picnic with Max and Daisy and Mum and Dad. Then they drove on a little further, and Kevin tried again, soaring up, up, up—but he still couldn't see his nest. So they drove a bit further, and then Kevin flew up for a third time, higher than ever, until the car looked like a toy on the ground far below.

And there, beyond the road, across
a white rushing river, behind a rocky
outcrop on one of the very highest of the
wild, wet hills he saw his own dear tree,
and the remains of his nest.

He let out a happy neigh. When Max
heard it he felt terribly happy, because he
knew Kevin had found his home, and also
terribly sad, because it meant that Kevin
would be leaving.

Kevin came swooping down again. He
hovered just above the car, ruffling Max's
hair with the flapping of his little wings.

He reached out his velvety nose and nuzzled Max's face. 'Bye, Max!' he whinnied, and Max fed him one last custard cream. Then Kevin flew right around the car three times, did a loop-the-loop, and flew away.

Max shaded his eyes against the evening sun and watched until Kevin looked no bigger than a bird. He watched until Kevin looked no bigger than a bee. He watched until Kevin vanished completely. And even then he kept on watching, just in case Kevin changed his mind and came back.

But Kevin did not come back, and after a while it started to get dark, and Mum said kindly, 'Come on, Max,' and Dad said, 'It's time we were getting back.'

Even Daisy was nice to him on the long drive home. But Max knew that it wouldn't feel like home at all without a roly-poly flying pony on the roof.

Back in his tree, Kevin carefully rebuilt his nest. He lined it with moss and lichen and snuggled down in it. He was happy to be back in his own hills. It felt good to be able to hear the wind blowing through the grass again, and the river laughing at its own jokes down in the valley, and all the other nature-noises which were

mostly drowned out
by people-sounds
in Bumbleford. This is
where I belong, he thought,
tucking his nose under his wing
and settling down to sleep.

But something had changed.
The woods and the winds and
the water weren't enough
for him any more. He
was missing something, and it wasn't just
custard creams. He was missing his Max.

Meanwhile, back in Bumbleford, Max was missing Kevin just as badly. He tried to be cheerful about it and tell himself that he had done a good thing by letting Kevin go back to the wild. But it had been so nice to listen to Kevin's little hooves clip-clopping about on the roof, and the room seemed very quiet without them. It had been so nice to wake up every morning and go running upstairs to see Kevin, and it was hard to get to sleep knowing that you would never ever have that to look forward to again.

Max felt as if there was a hole inside him, and it was a hole in the shape of a fat flying pony with very small wings.

◡ ∪ ◡

When he woke, the sun was shining through the curtains and the birds were singing. Something was going '**CLIP-CLOP**' above his ceiling, and Max thought sleepily, 'Kevin's awake.' Then he remembered that Kevin wasn't there any more, and felt sad all over again.

'**CLIP-CLOP**,' went the noises. '**CLIP-CLOP**.'

'Kevin?' whispered Max, throwing off the duvet.

'Kevin??' said Max, jumping out of bed.

'Kevin!!!' yelled Max, running out of the flat and up the stairs to the roof, in his pyjamas.

Kevin was standing on the roof, munching a mouthful of grass from the flowerpots. He had made himself a big raggedy nest near the pigeon coop and lined it with moss and pigeon feathers. He had had trouble getting to sleep, too. He'd had a long think, and he had decided that now he knew his way from Bumbleford to the wild, wet hills he could always go back there when he felt like it, or when Max was busy at school. The rest of the time, he could live on Max's roof. He had decided that home was wherever Max was.

But he didn't know enough words to explain all that to Max, so he just said, 'Custard creams?'